W9-CZK-984

My Little Pony™

Pony Tales

featuring

TWILIGHT SPARKLE

STORY, ART, and LETTERS BY Thomas Zahler

COLORS BY Ronda Pattison

ABDO Spotlight

IDW

ABDOPUBLISHING.COM

Reinforced library bound edition published in 2015 by Spotlight,
a division of ABDO, PO Box 398166, Minneapolis, Minnesota 55439.
Spotlight produces high-quality reinforced library bound editions for
schools and libraries. Published by agreement with IDW.

Printed in the United States of America, North Mankato, Minnesota.
112014
012015

THIS BOOK CONTAINS
RECYCLED MATERIALS

LIBRARY OF CONGRESS CATALOGING-IN-PUBLICATION DATA

Zahler, Thomas F., author, illustrator.
  Twilight Sparkle / writer, Thomas Zahler ; artist, Thomas Zahler. --
Reinforced library bound edition.
      pages cm. -- (My little pony. Pony tales)
  Summary: "Twilight Sparkle takes a job as the Archivist's assistant"--
Provided by publisher.
  ISBN 978-1-61479-336-6
1. Graphic novels. I. Title.
  PZ7.7.Z35Tw 2015
  741.5'973--dc23

                      2014036756

Spotlight

A Division of ABDO
abdopublishing.com

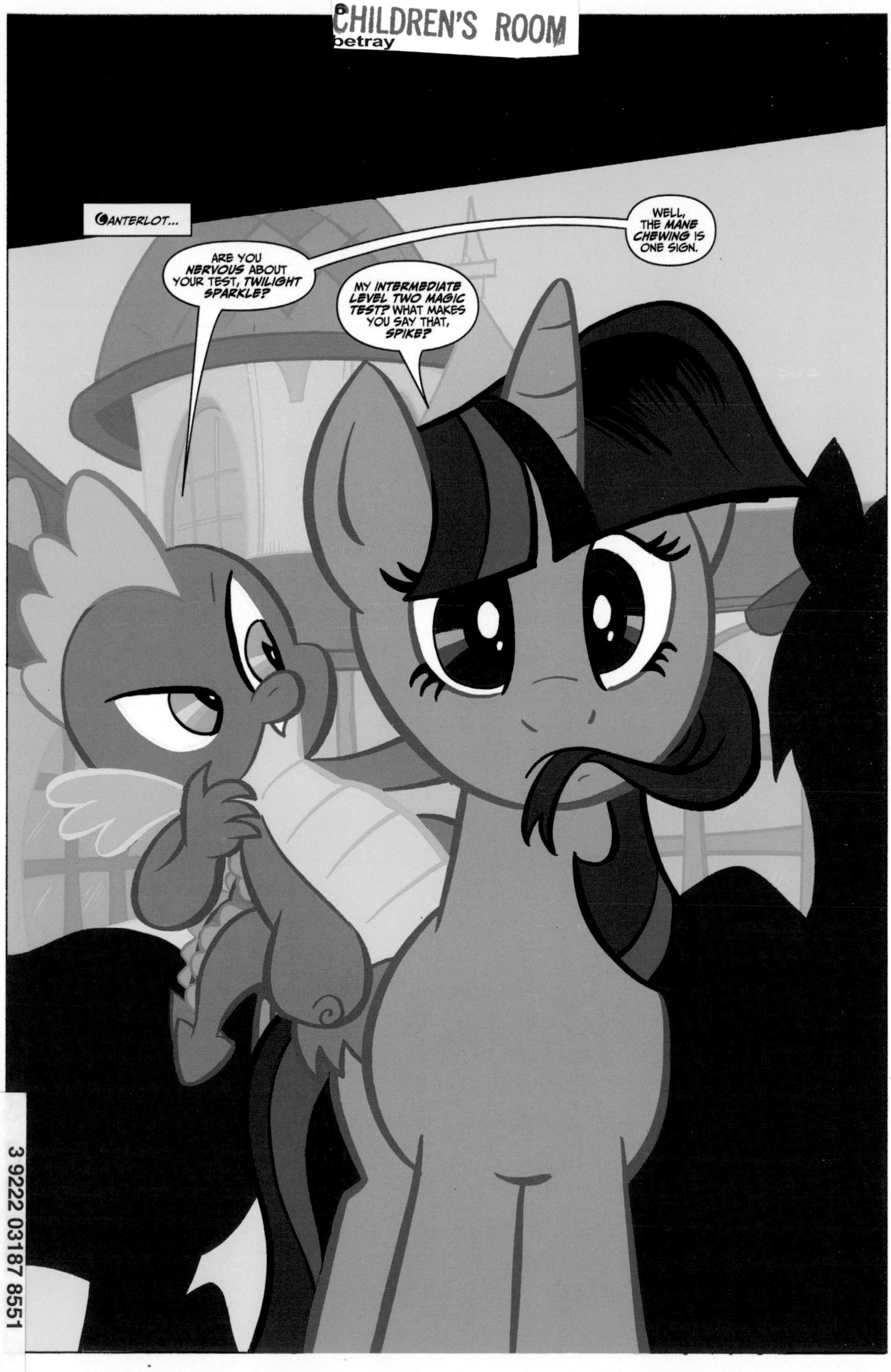
CANTERLOT...
ARE YOU NERVOUS ABOUT YOUR TEST, TWILIGHT SPARKLE?
MY INTERMEDIATE LEVEL TWO MAGIC TEST? WHAT MAKES YOU SAY THAT, SPIKE?
WELL, THE MANE CHEWING IS ONE SIGN.

AND WE'VE BEEN STANDING AT THE TOP OF THESE STAIRS FOR ALMOST *HALF AN HOUR.*

I HAPPEN TO *LIKE* THE VIEW OF *CANTERLOT* FROM HERE. AND I--

--OH, *WHO* AM I KIDDING? IT'S ONLY THE *HUGEST TEST* **EVER!**

YEAH, IT'S *PRETTY BAD.* IN FACT, THERE'S ONLY *ONE* THING I CAN THINK OF *WORSE* THAN THAT.

BEING *LATE.*

WHAT?

POOF!

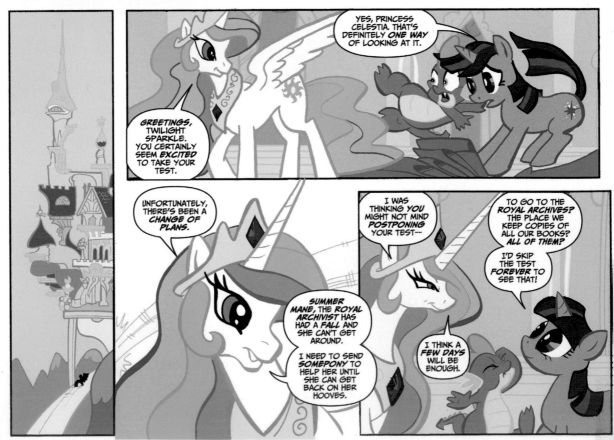

YES, PRINCESS CELESTIA. THAT'S DEFINITELY *ONE WAY* OF LOOKING AT IT.

GREETINGS, TWILIGHT SPARKLE. YOU CERTAINLY SEEM *EXCITED* TO TAKE YOUR TEST.

UNFORTUNATELY, THERE'S BEEN A *CHANGE OF PLANS.*

I WAS THINKING *YOU* MIGHT NOT MIND *POSTPONING* YOUR TEST--

SUMMER MANE, THE *ROYAL ARCHIVIST* HAS HAD A *FALL* AND SHE CAN'T GET AROUND.

I NEED TO SEND *SOMEPONY* TO HELP HER UNTIL SHE CAN GET BACK ON HER HOOVES.

TO GO TO THE *ROYAL ARCHIVES?* THE PLACE WE KEEP COPIES OF ALL OUR BOOKS? *ALL OF THEM?*

I'D SKIP THE TEST *FOREVER* TO SEE THAT!

I THINK A *FEW DAYS* WILL BE ENOUGH.

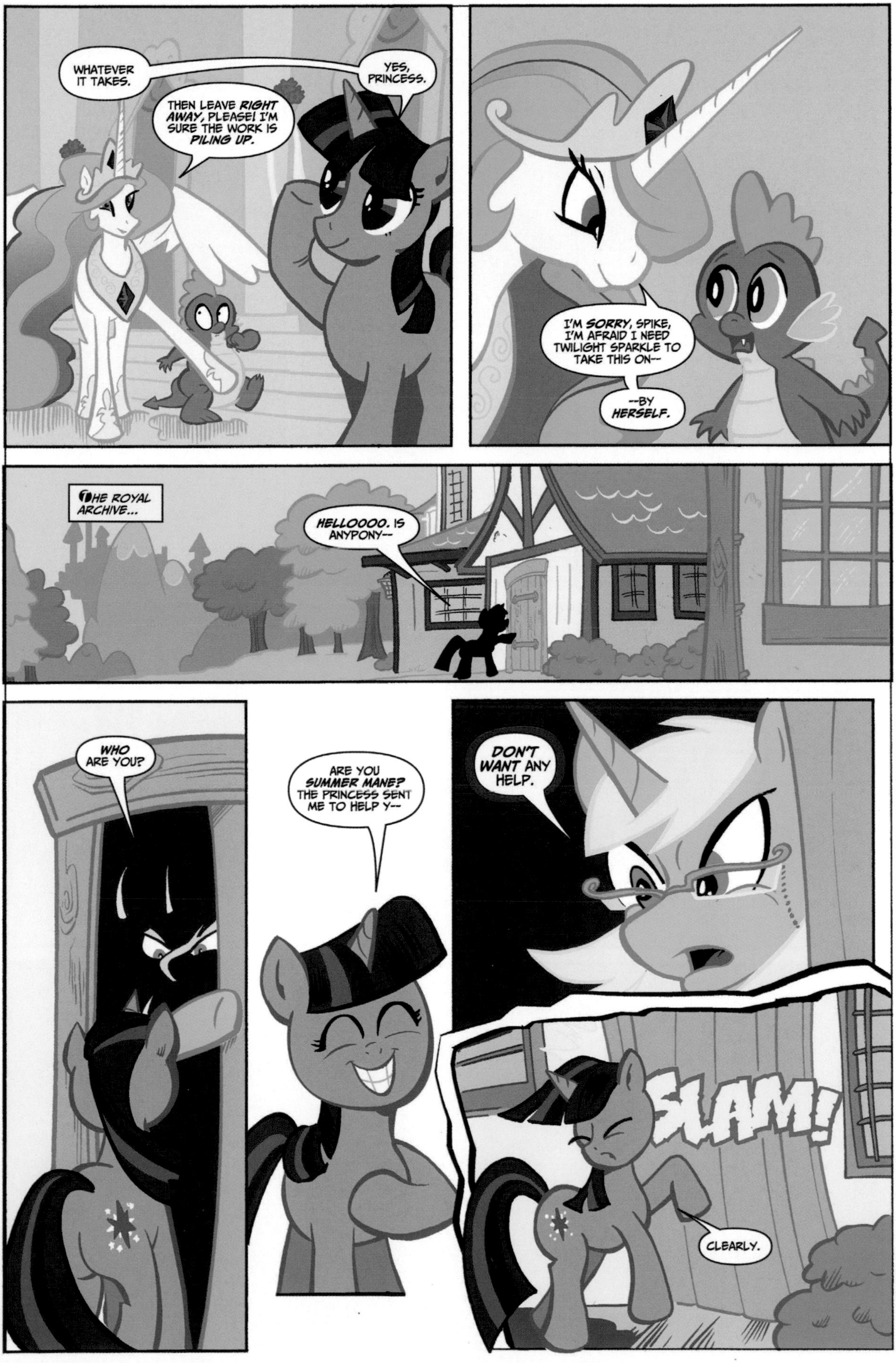
WHATEVER IT TAKES.
YES, PRINCESS.
THEN LEAVE RIGHT AWAY, PLEASE! I'M SURE THE WORK IS PILING UP.
I'M SORRY, SPIKE, I'M AFRAID I NEED TWILIGHT SPARKLE TO TAKE THIS ON--
--BY HERSELF.
THE ROYAL ARCHIVE...
HELLOOOO. IS ANYPONY--
WHO ARE YOU?
ARE YOU SUMMER MANE? THE PRINCESS SENT ME TO HELP Y--
DON'T WANT ANY HELP.
SLAM!
CLEARLY.

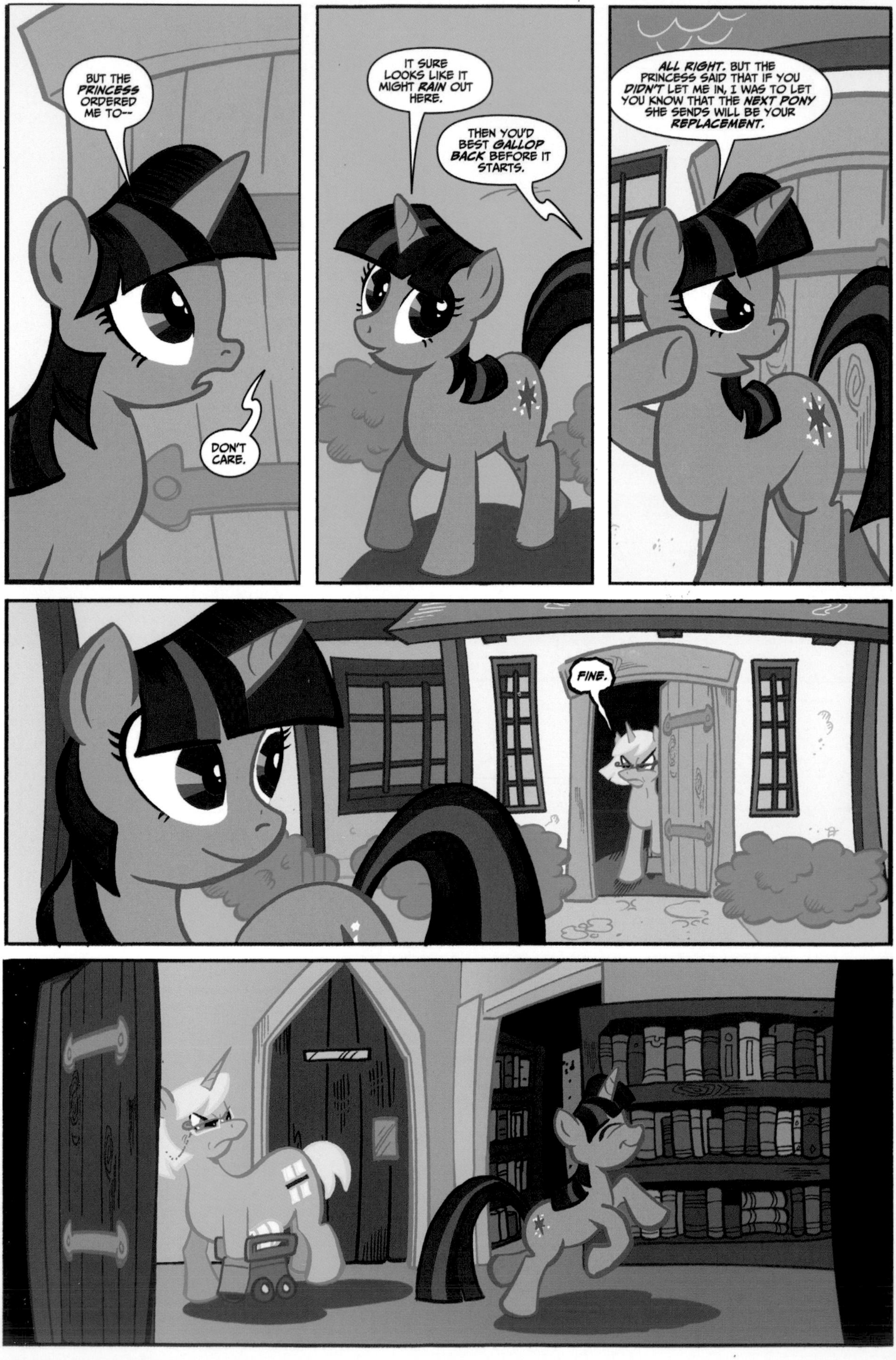

BUT THE PRINCESS ORDERED ME TO--
DON'T CARE.
IT SURE LOOKS LIKE IT MIGHT RAIN OUT HERE.
THEN YOU'D BEST GALLOP BACK BEFORE IT STARTS.
ALL RIGHT. BUT THE PRINCESS SAID THAT IF YOU DIDN'T LET ME IN, I WAS TO LET YOU KNOW THAT THE NEXT PONY SHE SENDS WILL BE YOUR REPLACEMENT.
FINE.

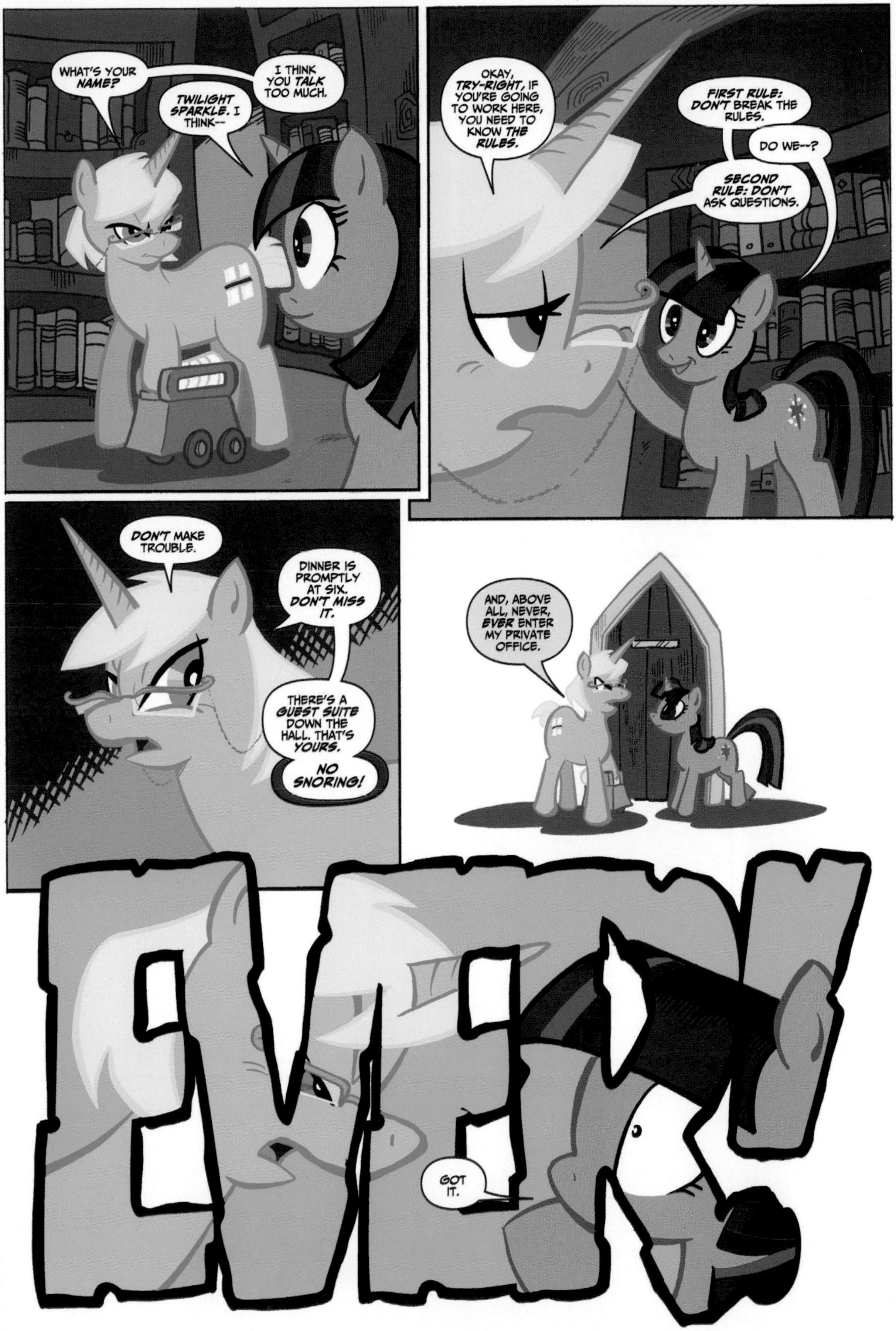
WHAT'S YOUR NAME?
TWILIGHT SPARKLE. I THINK--
I THINK YOU TALK TOO MUCH.
OKAY, TRY-RIGHT, IF YOU'RE GOING TO WORK HERE, YOU NEED TO KNOW THE RULES.
FIRST RULE: DON'T BREAK THE RULES.
DO WE--?
SECOND RULE: DON'T ASK QUESTIONS.
DON'T MAKE TROUBLE.
DINNER IS PROMPTLY AT SIX. DON'T MISS IT.
THERE'S A GUEST SUITE DOWN THE HALL. THAT'S YOURS.
NO SNORING!
AND, ABOVE ALL, NEVER, EVER ENTER MY PRIVATE OFFICE.
EVER!
GOT IT.

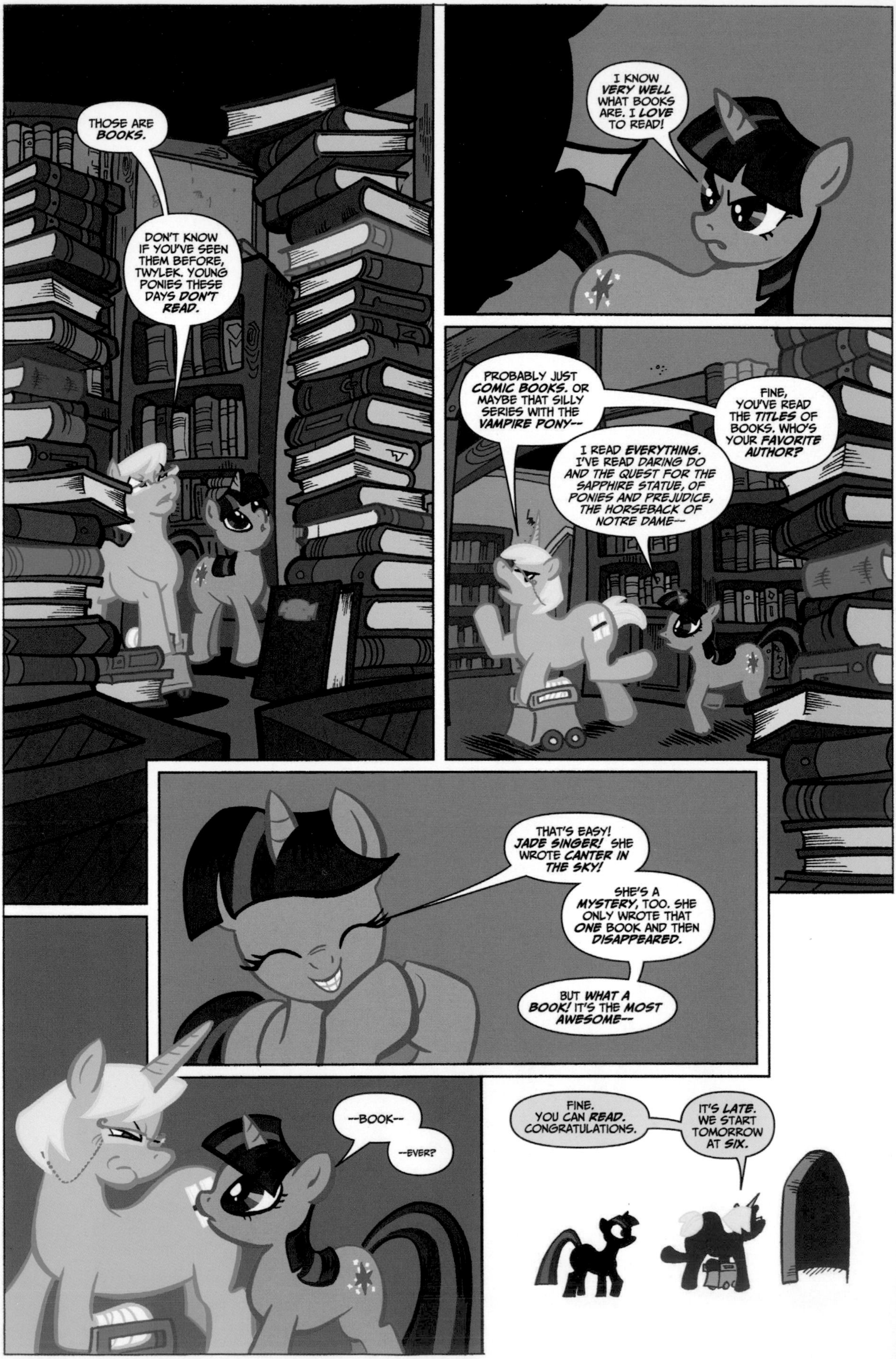
THOSE ARE BOOKS.
DON'T KNOW IF YOU'VE SEEN THEM BEFORE, TWYLEK. YOUNG PONIES THESE DAYS DON'T READ.
I KNOW VERY WELL WHAT BOOKS ARE. I LOVE TO READ!
PROBABLY JUST COMIC BOOKS. OR MAYBE THAT SILLY SERIES WITH THE VAMPIRE PONY--
I READ EVERYTHING. I'VE READ DARING DO AND THE QUEST FOR THE SAPPHIRE STATUE, OF PONIES AND PREJUDICE, THE HORSEBACK OF NOTRE DAME--
FINE, YOU'VE READ THE TITLES OF BOOKS. WHO'S YOUR FAVORITE AUTHOR?
THAT'S EASY! JADE SINGER! SHE WROTE CANTER IN THE SKY!
SHE'S A MYSTERY, TOO. SHE ONLY WROTE THAT ONE BOOK AND THEN DISAPPEARED.
BUT WHAT A BOOK! IT'S THE MOST AWESOME--
--BOOK--
--EVER?
FINE. YOU CAN READ. CONGRATULATIONS.
IT'S LATE. WE START TOMORROW AT SIX.

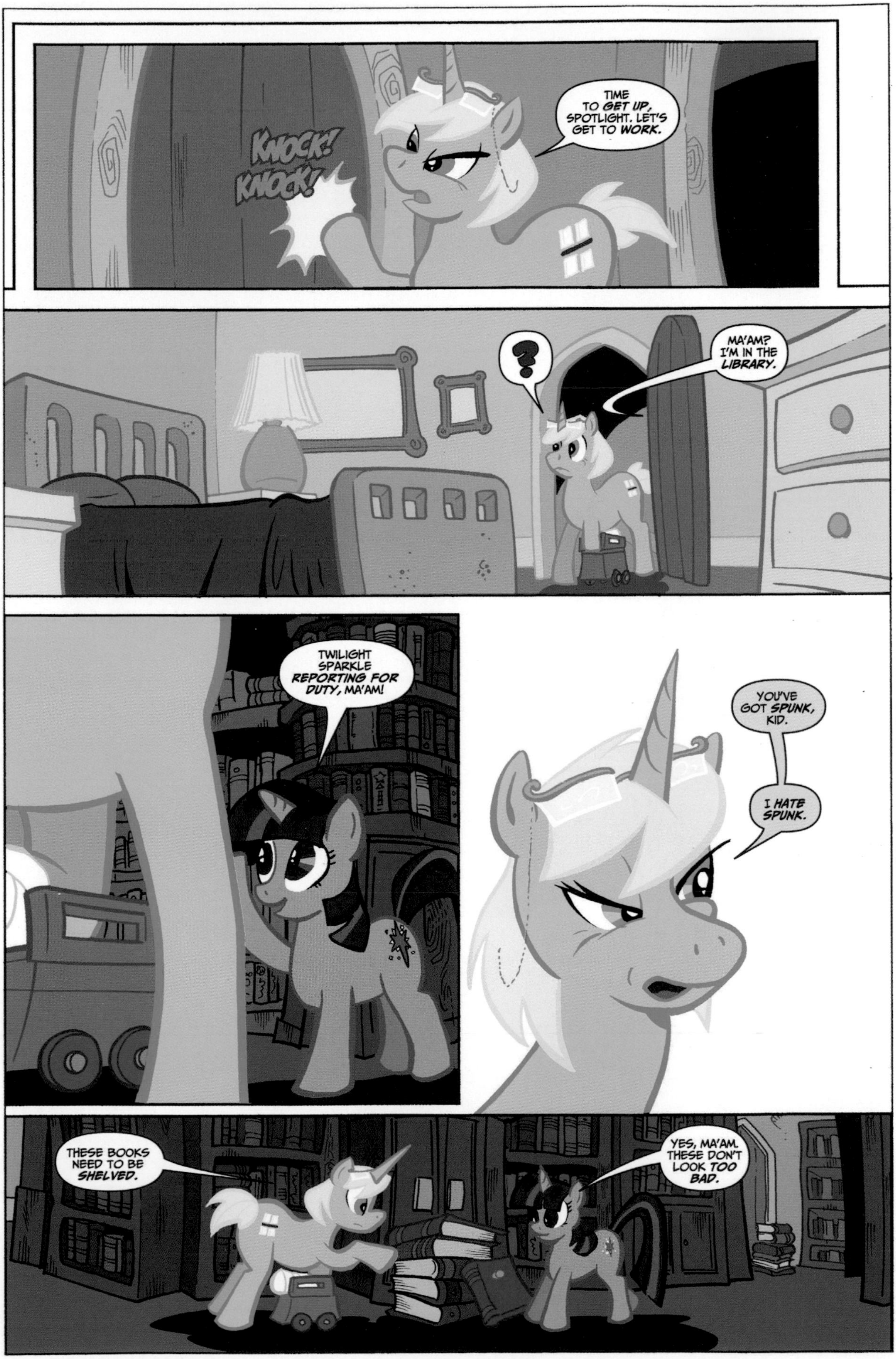
KNOCK! KNOCK!
TIME TO GET UP, SPOTLIGHT. LET'S GET TO WORK.
?
MA'AM? I'M IN THE LIBRARY.
TWILIGHT SPARKLE REPORTING FOR DUTY, MA'AM!
YOU'VE GOT SPUNK, KID.
I HATE SPUNK.
THESE BOOKS NEED TO BE SHELVED.
YES, MA'AM. THESE DON'T LOOK TOO BAD.

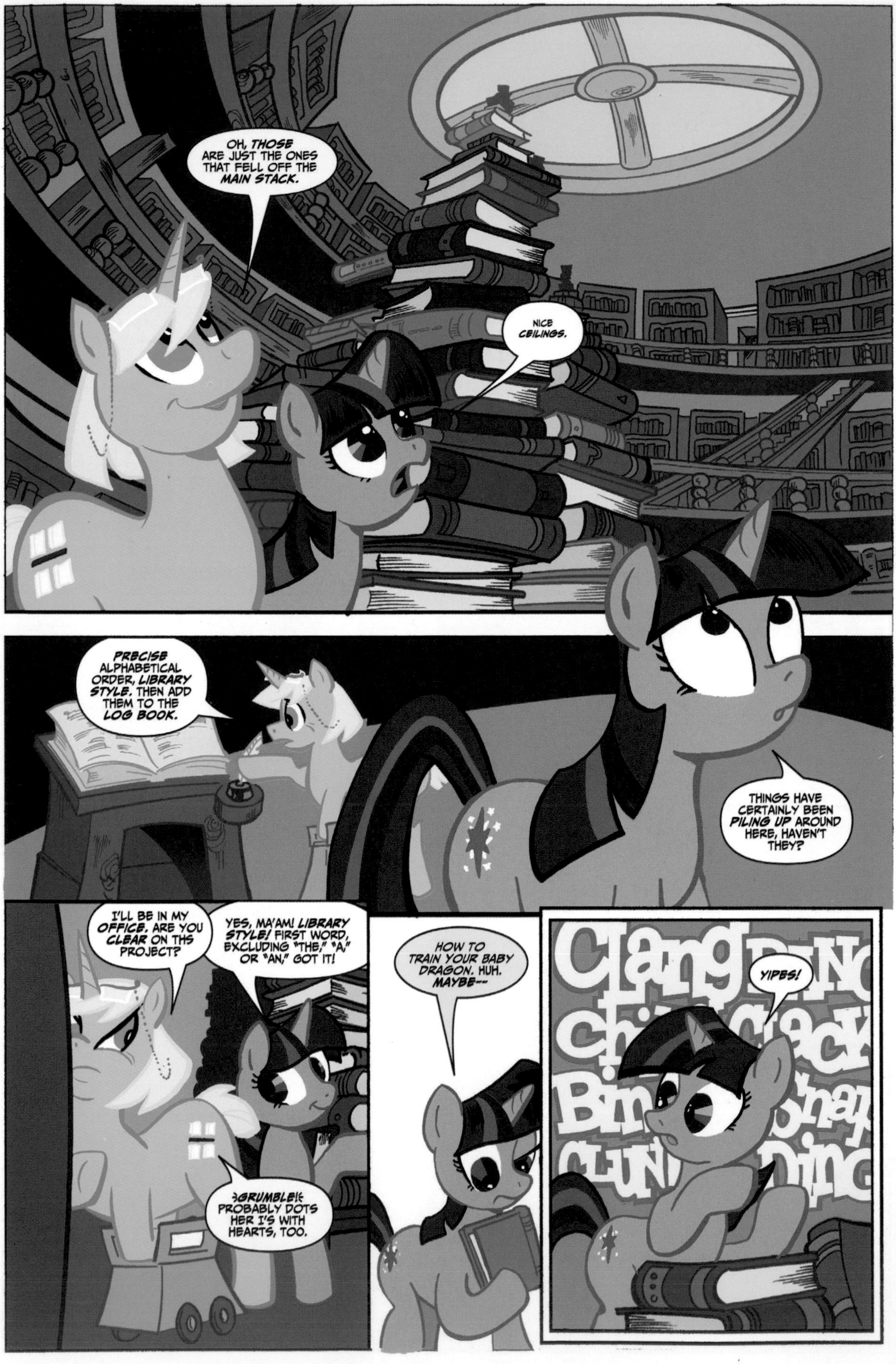

OH, THOSE ARE JUST THE ONES THAT FELL OFF THE MAIN STACK.
NICE CEILINGS.
PRECISE ALPHABETICAL ORDER, LIBRARY STYLE. THEN ADD THEM TO THE LOG BOOK.
THINGS HAVE CERTAINLY BEEN PILING UP AROUND HERE, HAVEN'T THEY?
I'LL BE IN MY OFFICE. ARE YOU CLEAR ON THS PROJECT?
YES, MA'AM! LIBRARY STYLE! FIRST WORD, EXCLUDING "THE," "A," OR "AN," GOT IT!
GRUMBLE! PROBABLY DOTS HER I'S WITH HEARTS, TOO.
HOW TO TRAIN YOUR BABY DRAGON. HUH. MAYBE--
YIPES!

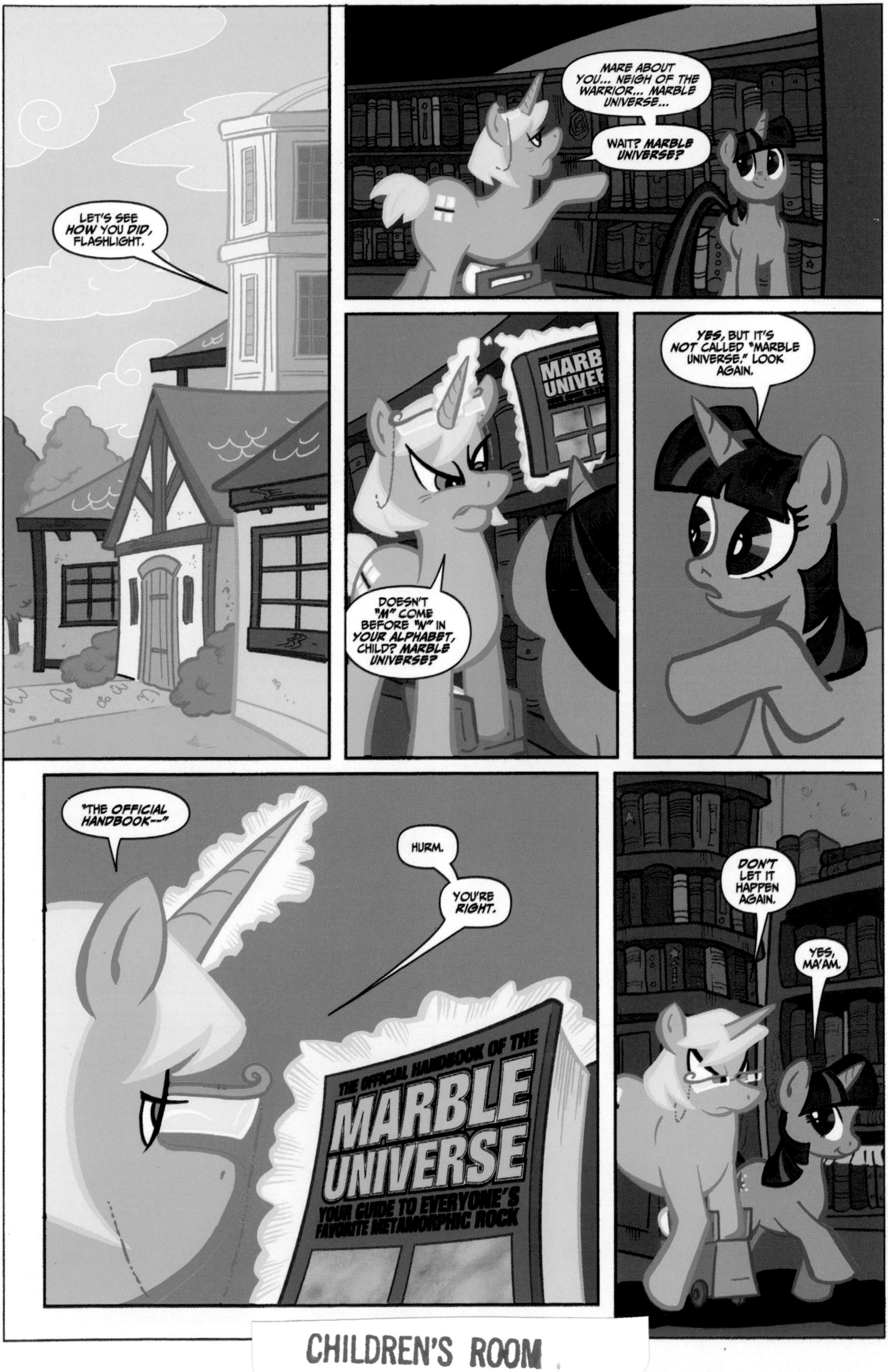
LET'S SEE HOW YOU DID, FLASHLIGHT.
MARE ABOUT YOU... NEIGH OF THE WARRIOR... MARBLE UNIVERSE...
WAIT? MARBLE UNIVERSE?
DOESN'T "M" COME BEFORE "W" IN YOUR ALPHABET, CHILD? MARBLE UNIVERSE?
YES, BUT IT'S NOT CALLED "MARBLE UNIVERSE." LOOK AGAIN.
"THE OFFICIAL HANDBOOK--"
HURM.
YOU'RE RIGHT.
THE OFFICIAL HANDBOOK OF THE MARBLE UNIVERSE YOUR GUIDE TO EVERYONE'S FAVORITE METAMORPHIC ROCK
DON'T LET IT HAPPEN AGAIN.
YES, MA'AM.
CHILDREN'S ROOM

DID YOU--
--EVER--
--NEVER MIND.
WHAT DID--
GULP!
SO, TWYLEK, WHAT ARE YOU READING?

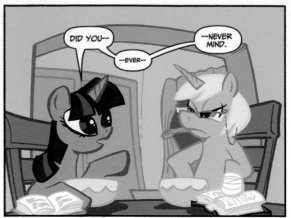

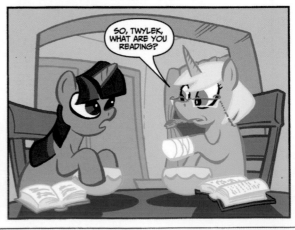

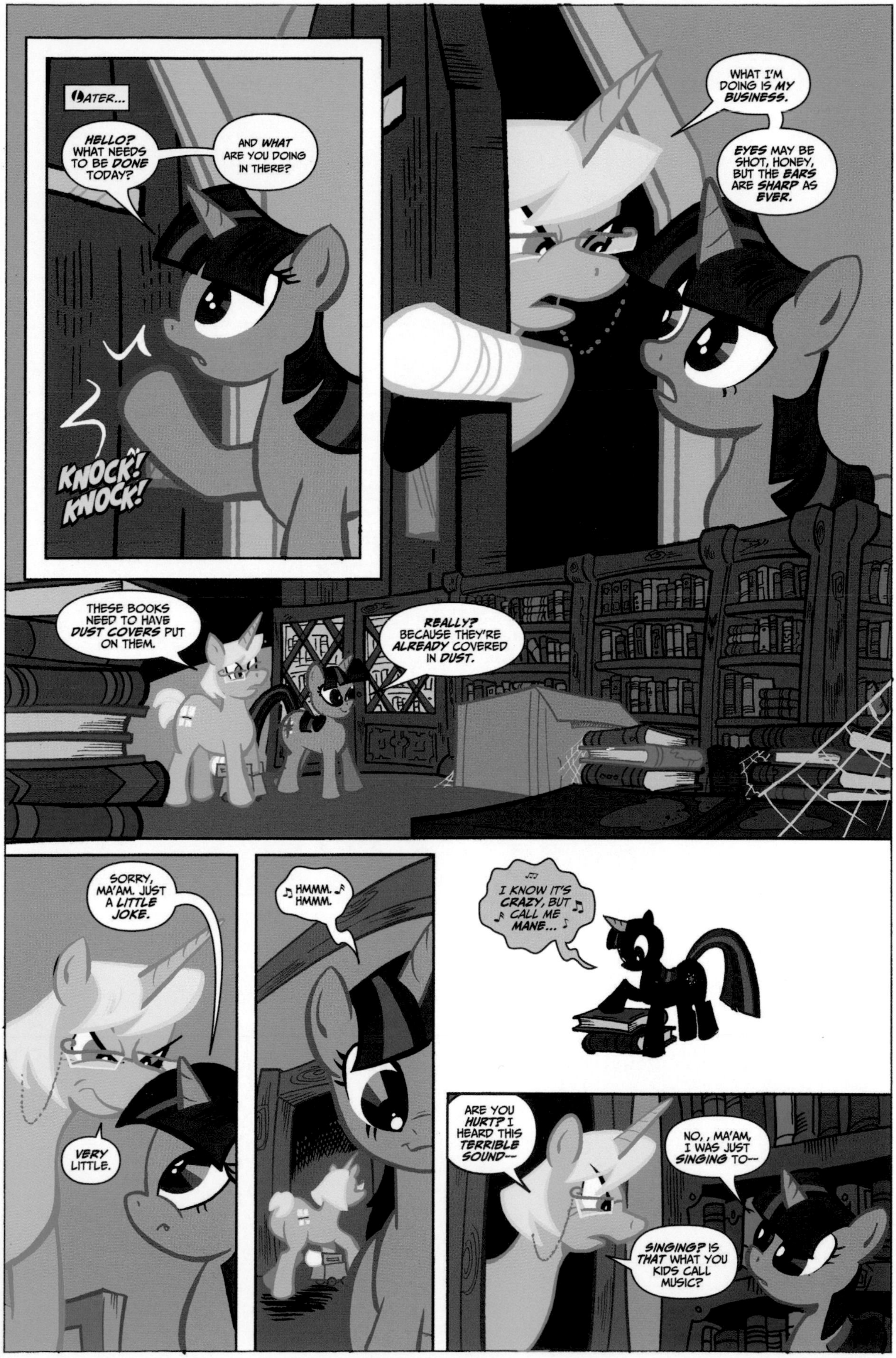

LATER...
HELLO? WHAT NEEDS TO BE DONE TODAY?
AND WHAT ARE YOU DOING IN THERE?
KNOCK! KNOCK!
WHAT I'M DOING IS MY BUSINESS.
EYES MAY BE SHOT, HONEY, BUT THE EARS ARE SHARP AS EVER.
THESE BOOKS NEED TO HAVE DUST COVERS PUT ON THEM.
REALLY? BECAUSE THEY'RE ALREADY COVERED IN DUST.
SORRY, MA'AM. JUST A LITTLE JOKE.
VERY LITTLE.
HMMM. HMMM.
I KNOW IT'S CRAZY, BUT CALL ME MANE...
ARE YOU HURT? I HEARD THIS TERRIBLE SOUND--
NO, , MA'AM, I WAS JUST SINGING TO--
SINGING? IS THAT WHAT YOU KIDS CALL MUSIC?

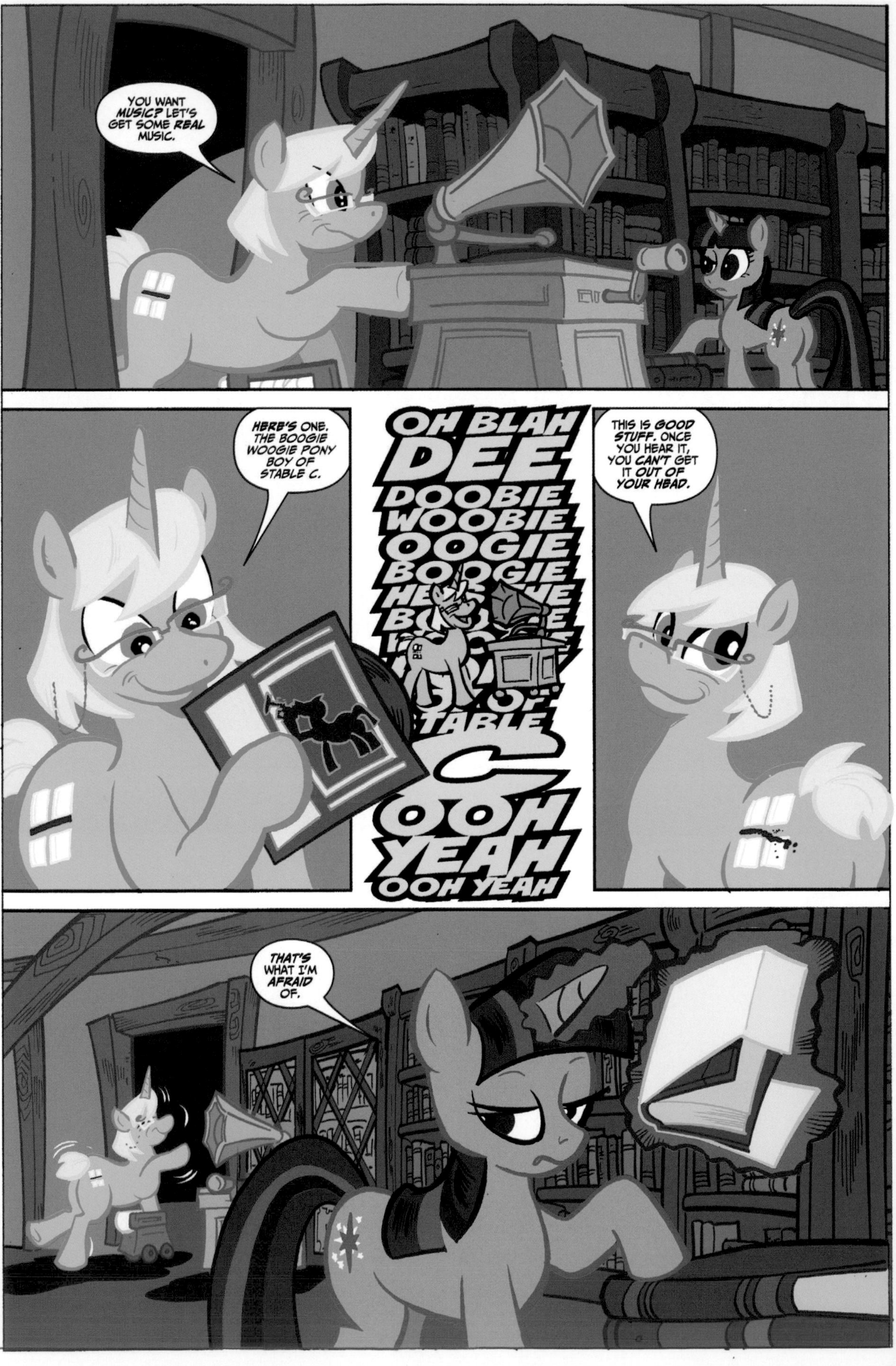
YOU WANT MUSIC? LET'S GET SOME REAL MUSIC.
HERE'S ONE. THE BOOGIE WOOGIE PONY BOY OF STABLE C.
OH BLAH DEE DOOBIE WOOBIE OOGIE BOOGIE
TABLE C OOH YEAH OOH YEAH
THIS IS GOOD STUFF. ONCE YOU HEAR IT, YOU CAN'T GET IT OUT OF YOUR HEAD.
THAT'S WHAT I'M AFRAID OF.

A BIT LATER...

--NO, SHE WROTE THAT ONE OUT *LONGHAND.*

NO WAY! I THOUGHT *EVERYONE* USED A TYPEWRITER.

A *LOT* DO. IN FACT, SOME AUTHORS ARE *VERY PICKY* ABOUT THEIRS.

DO YOU KNOW WHAT *JADE SINGER* USED?

HMM. I THINK SHE USED AN OLD *LIPPONZONER* MODEL. I *DON'T KNOW.*

YOU'RE A LITTLE TOO *HOOKED* ON HER, YOU KNOW. HAVE YOU EVER READ ANYTHING BY *CESIUM GRANDE?*

NO, MA'AM.

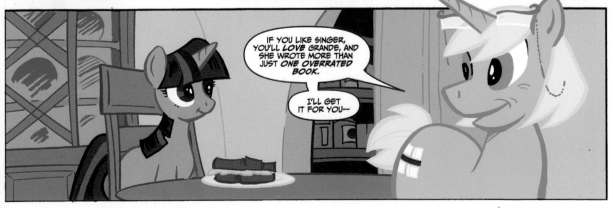

IF YOU LIKE SINGER, YOU'LL *LOVE* GRANDE, AND SHE WROTE MORE THAN JUST *ONE OVERRATED BOOK.*

I'LL GET IT FOR YOU--

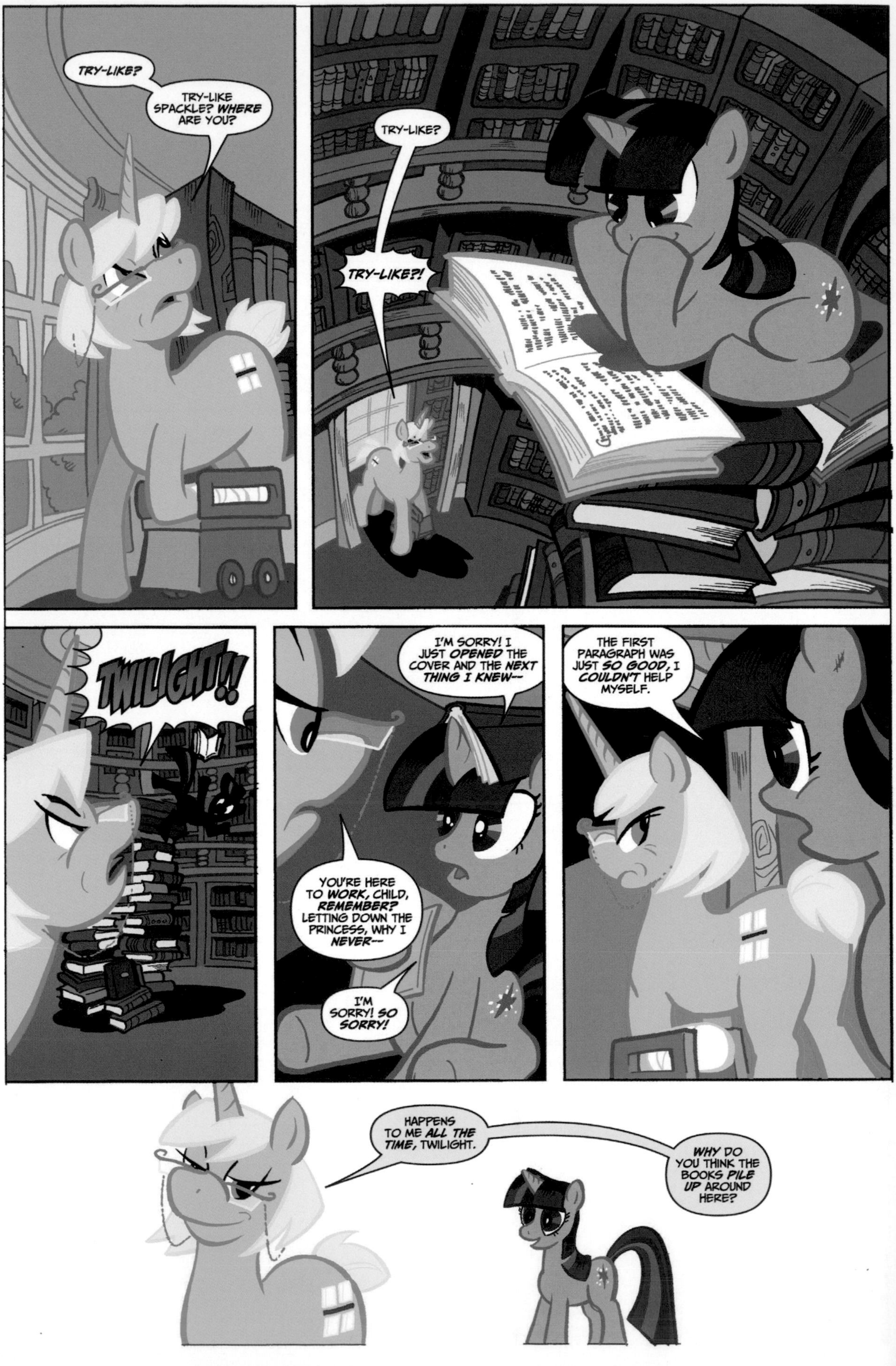
TRY-LIKE?
TRY-LIKE SPACKLE? WHERE ARE YOU?
TRY-LIKE?
TRY-LIKE?!
TWILIGHT!!
I'M SORRY! I JUST OPENED THE COVER AND THE NEXT THING I KNEW--
YOU'RE HERE TO WORK, CHILD, REMEMBER? LETTING DOWN THE PRINCESS, WHY I NEVER--
I'M SORRY! SO SORRY!
THE FIRST PARAGRAPH WAS JUST SO GOOD, I COULDN'T HELP MYSELF.
HAPPENS TO ME ALL THE TIME, TWILIGHT.
WHY DO YOU THINK THE BOOKS PILE UP AROUND HERE?

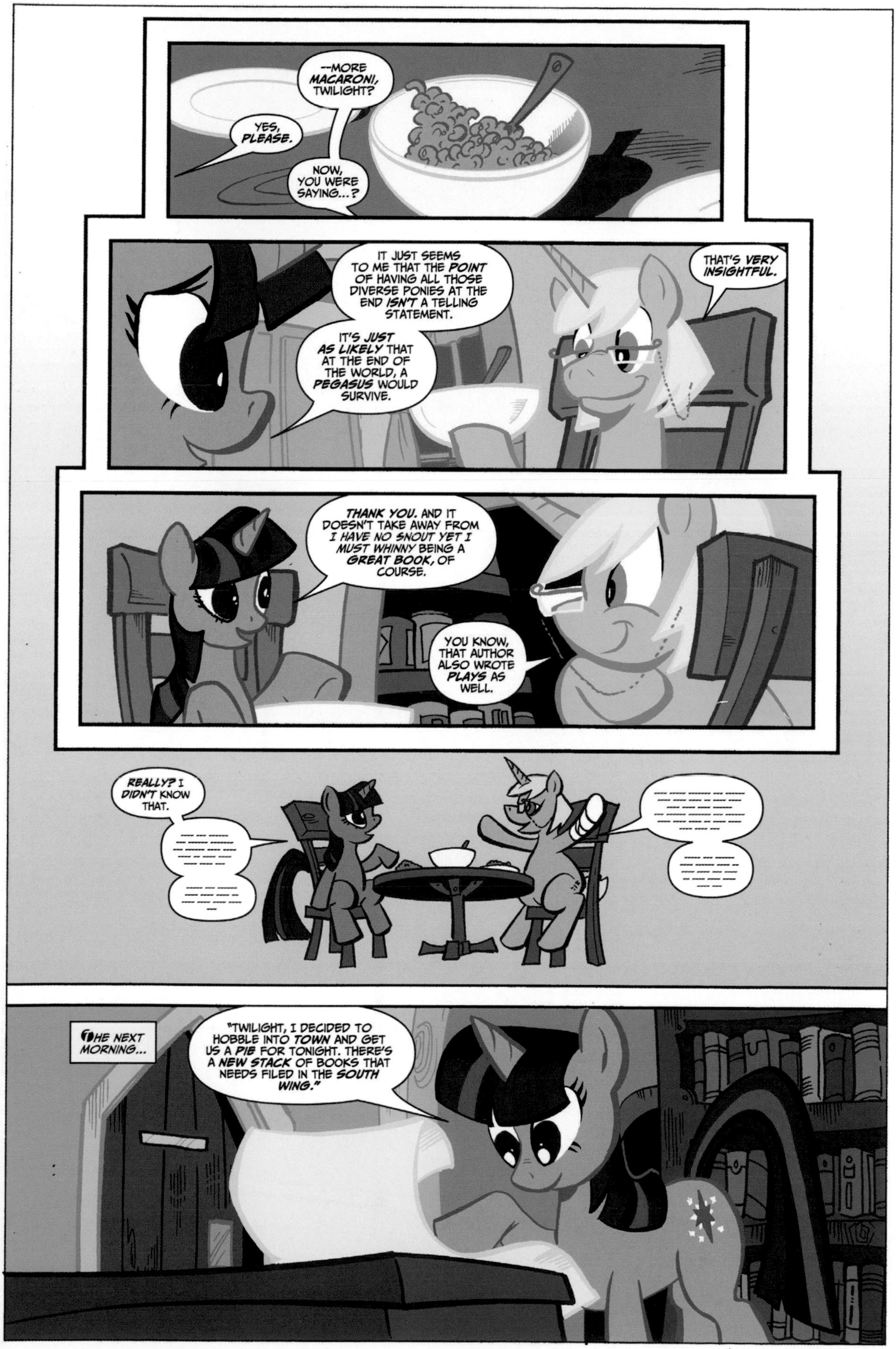
--MORE MACARONI, TWILIGHT?
YES, PLEASE.
NOW, YOU WERE SAYING...?
IT JUST SEEMS TO ME THAT THE POINT OF HAVING ALL THOSE DIVERSE PONIES AT THE END ISN'T A TELLING STATEMENT.
IT'S JUST AS LIKELY THAT AT THE END OF THE WORLD, A PEGASUS WOULD SURVIVE.
THAT'S VERY INSIGHTFUL.
THANK YOU. AND IT DOESN'T TAKE AWAY FROM I HAVE NO SNOUT YET I MUST WHINNY BEING A GREAT BOOK, OF COURSE.
YOU KNOW, THAT AUTHOR ALSO WROTE PLAYS AS WELL.
REALLY? I DIDN'T KNOW THAT.
THE NEXT MORNING...
"TWILIGHT, I DECIDED TO HOBBLE INTO TOWN AND GET US A PIE FOR TONIGHT. THERE'S A NEW STACK OF BOOKS THAT NEEDS FILED IN THE SOUTH WING."

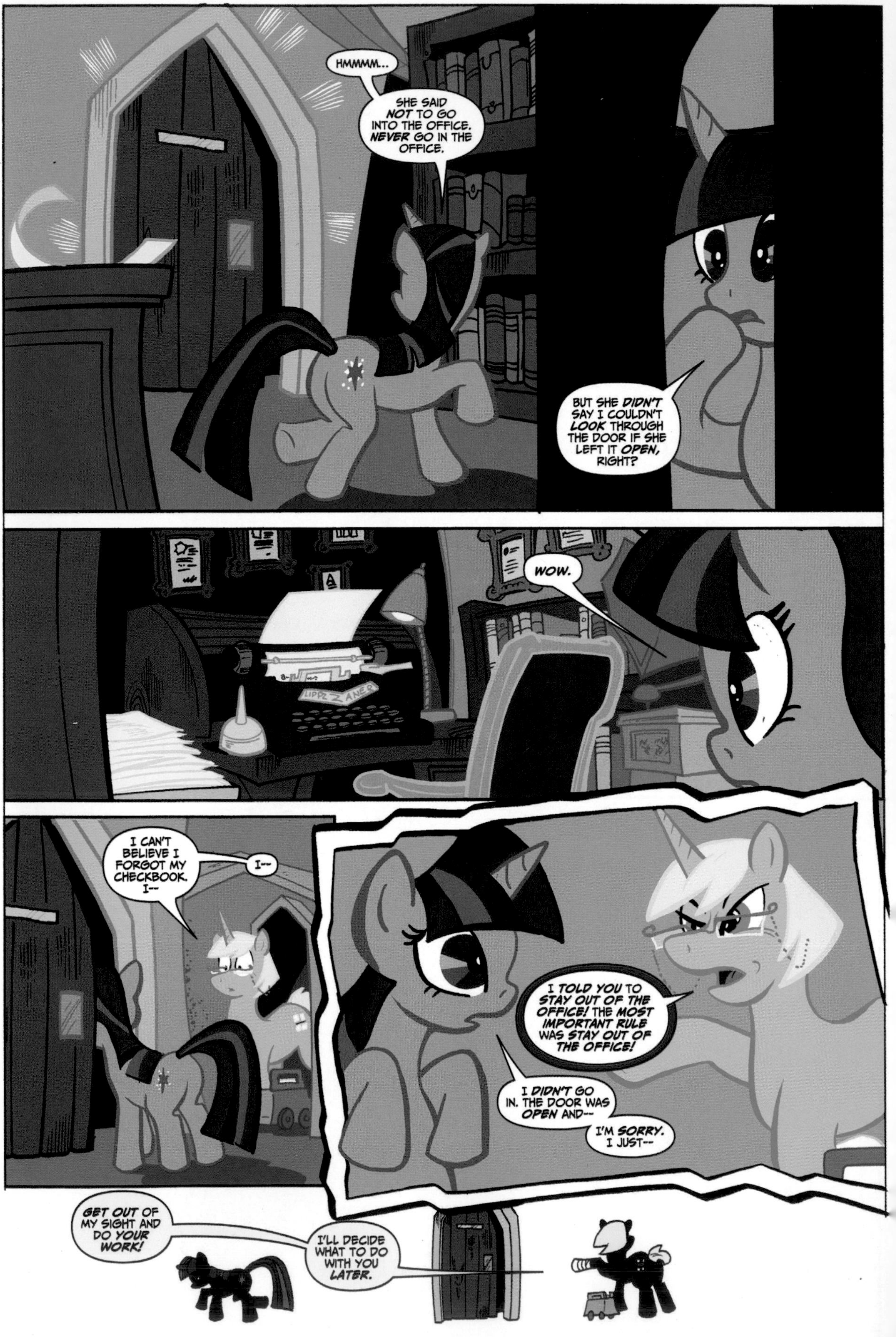

HMMMM...
SHE SAID NOT TO GO INTO THE OFFICE. NEVER GO IN THE OFFICE.
BUT SHE DIDN'T SAY I COULDN'T LOOK THROUGH THE DOOR IF SHE LEFT IT OPEN, RIGHT?
WOW.
LIPPZZANER
I CAN'T BELIEVE I FORGOT MY CHECKBOOK. I--
I--
I TOLD YOU TO STAY OUT OF THE OFFICE! THE MOST IMPORTANT RULE WAS STAY OUT OF THE OFFICE!
I DIDN'T GO IN. THE DOOR WAS OPEN AND--
I'M SORRY. I JUST--
GET OUT OF MY SIGHT AND DO YOUR WORK!
I'LL DECIDE WHAT TO DO WITH YOU LATER.

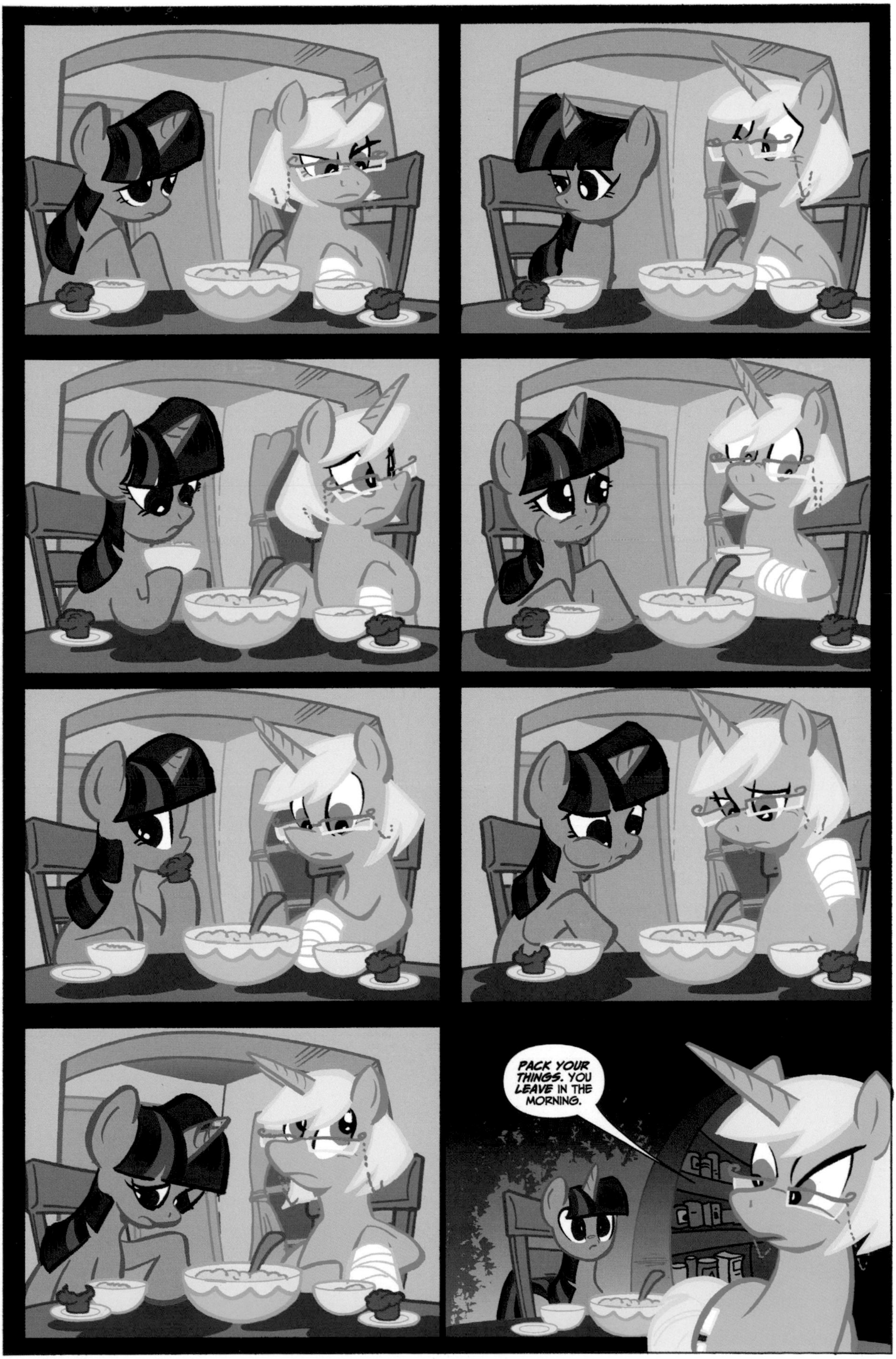
PACK YOUR THINGS. YOU LEAVE IN THE MORNING.

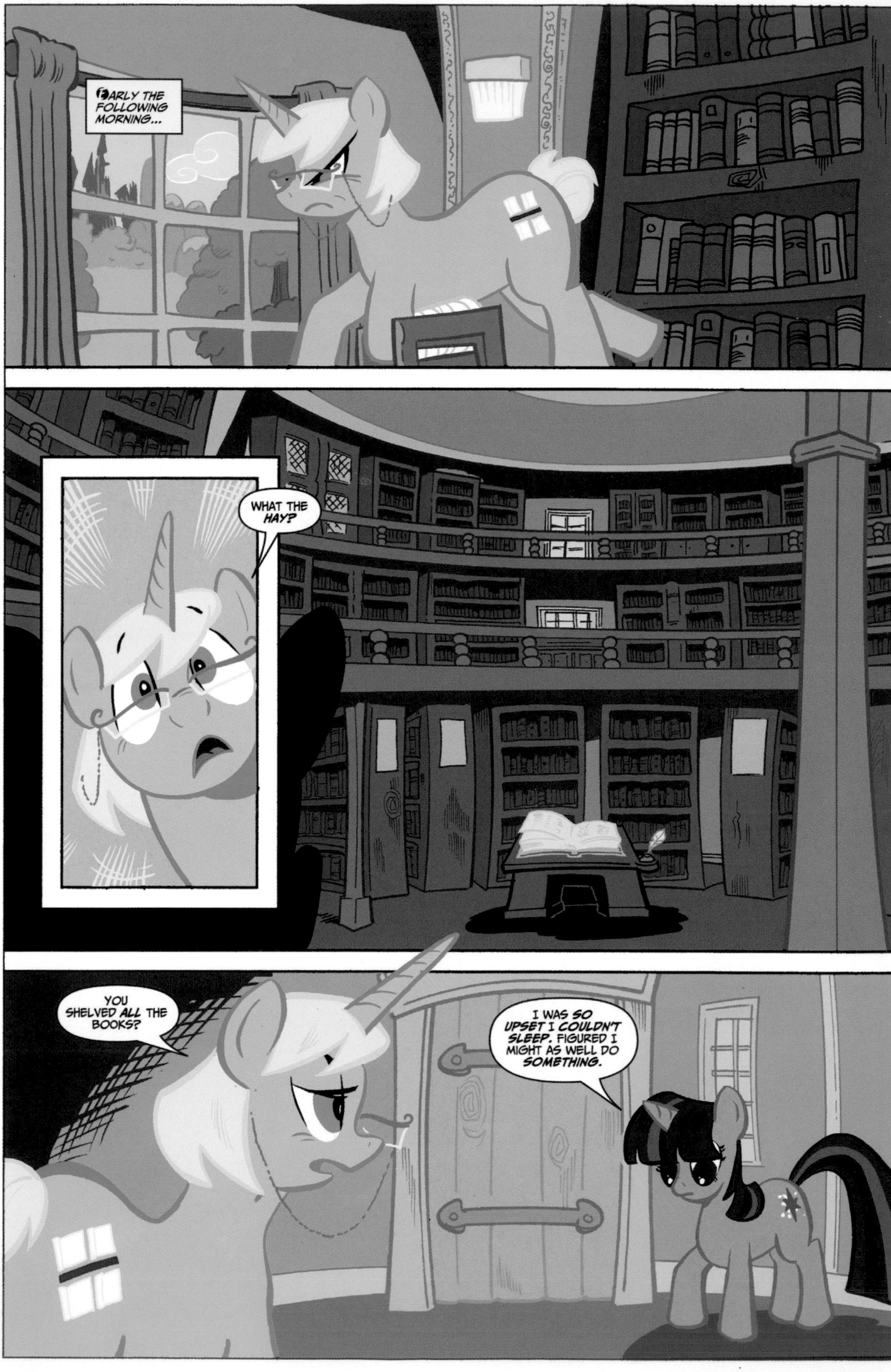
EARLY THE FOLLOWING MORNING...
WHAT THE HAY?
YOU SHELVED ALL THE BOOKS?
I WAS SO UPSET I COULDN'T SLEEP. FIGURED I MIGHT AS WELL DO SOMETHING.

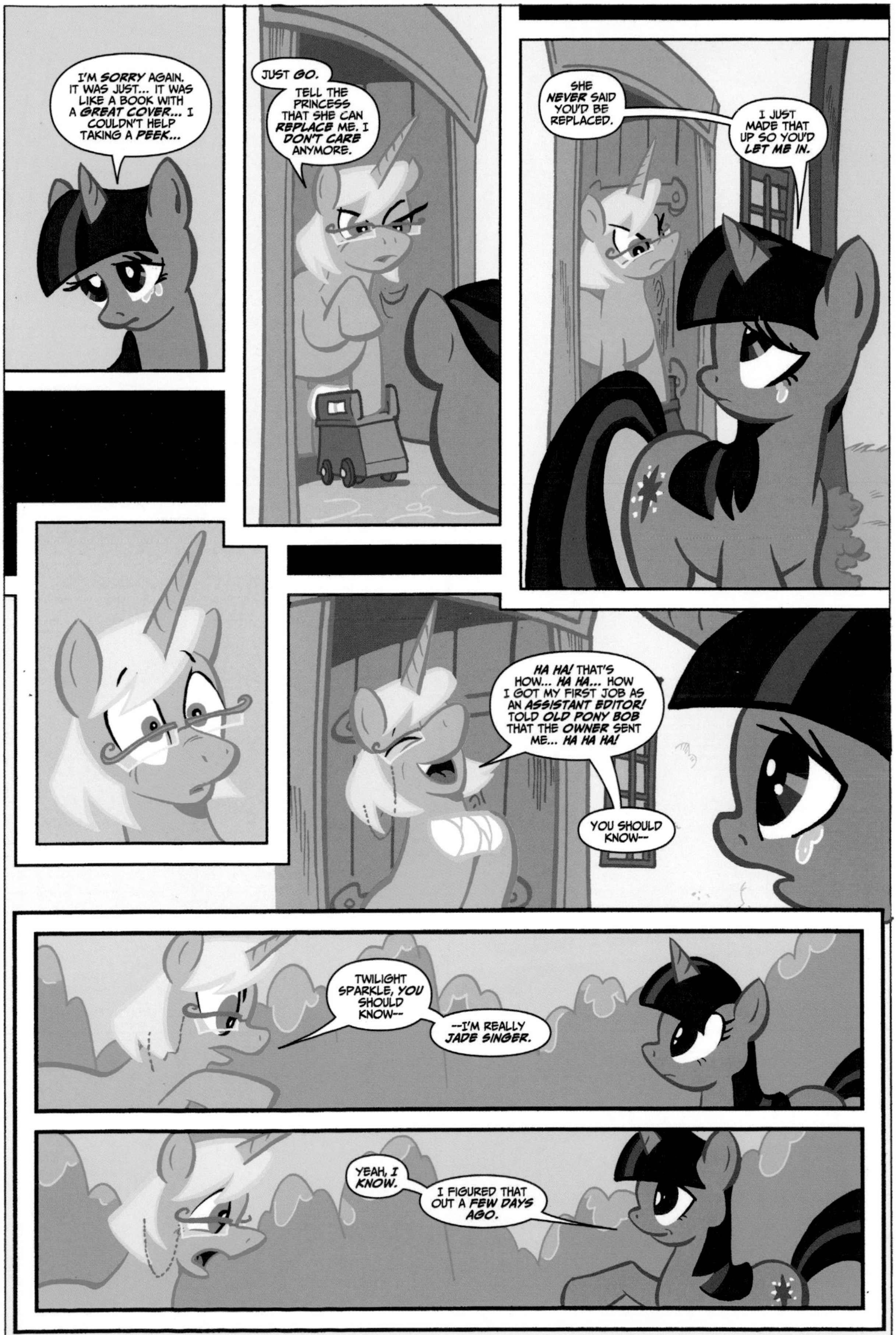
I'M SORRY AGAIN. IT WAS JUST... IT WAS LIKE A BOOK WITH A GREAT COVER... I COULDN'T HELP TAKING A PEEK...
JUST GO.
TELL THE PRINCESS THAT SHE CAN REPLACE ME. I DON'T CARE ANYMORE.
SHE NEVER SAID YOU'D BE REPLACED.
I JUST MADE THAT UP SO YOU'D LET ME IN.
HA HA! THAT'S HOW... HA HA... HOW I GOT MY FIRST JOB AS AN ASSISTANT EDITOR! TOLD OLD PONY BOB THAT THE OWNER SENT ME... HA HA HA!
YOU SHOULD KNOW--
TWILIGHT SPARKLE, YOU SHOULD KNOW--
--I'M REALLY JADE SINGER.
YEAH, I KNOW.
I FIGURED THAT OUT A FEW DAYS AGO.

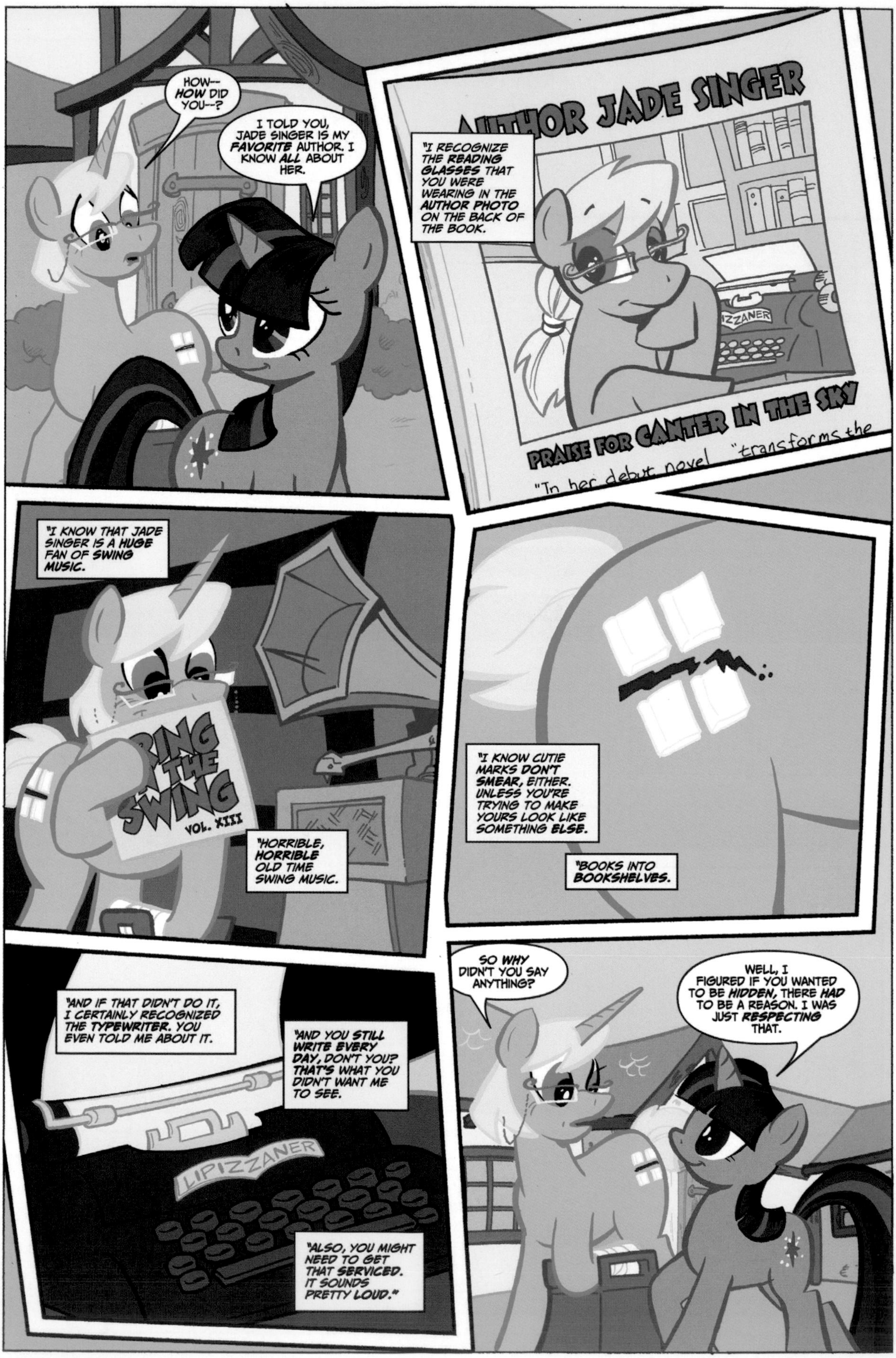
HOW-- HOW DID YOU--?
I TOLD YOU, JADE SINGER IS MY FAVORITE AUTHOR. I KNOW ALL ABOUT HER.
AUTHOR JADE SINGER
"I RECOGNIZE THE READING GLASSES THAT YOU WERE WEARING IN THE AUTHOR PHOTO ON THE BACK OF THE BOOK.
PRAISE FOR CANTER IN THE SKY
"In her debut novel "transforms the
"I KNOW THAT JADE SINGER IS A HUGE FAN OF SWING MUSIC.
VOL. XIII
"HORRIBLE, HORRIBLE OLD TIME SWING MUSIC.
"I KNOW CUTIE MARKS DON'T SMEAR, EITHER. UNLESS YOU'RE TRYING TO MAKE YOURS LOOK LIKE SOMETHING ELSE.
"BOOKS INTO BOOKSHELVES.
"AND IF THAT DIDN'T DO IT, I CERTAINLY RECOGNIZED THE TYPEWRITER. YOU EVEN TOLD ME ABOUT IT.
"AND YOU STILL WRITE EVERY DAY, DON'T YOU? THAT'S WHAT YOU DIDN'T WANT ME TO SEE.
LIPIZZANER
"ALSO, YOU MIGHT NEED TO GET THAT SERVICED. IT SOUNDS PRETTY LOUD."
SO WHY DIDN'T YOU SAY ANYTHING?
WELL, I FIGURED IF YOU WANTED TO BE HIDDEN, THERE HAD TO BE A REASON. I WAS JUST RESPECTING THAT.

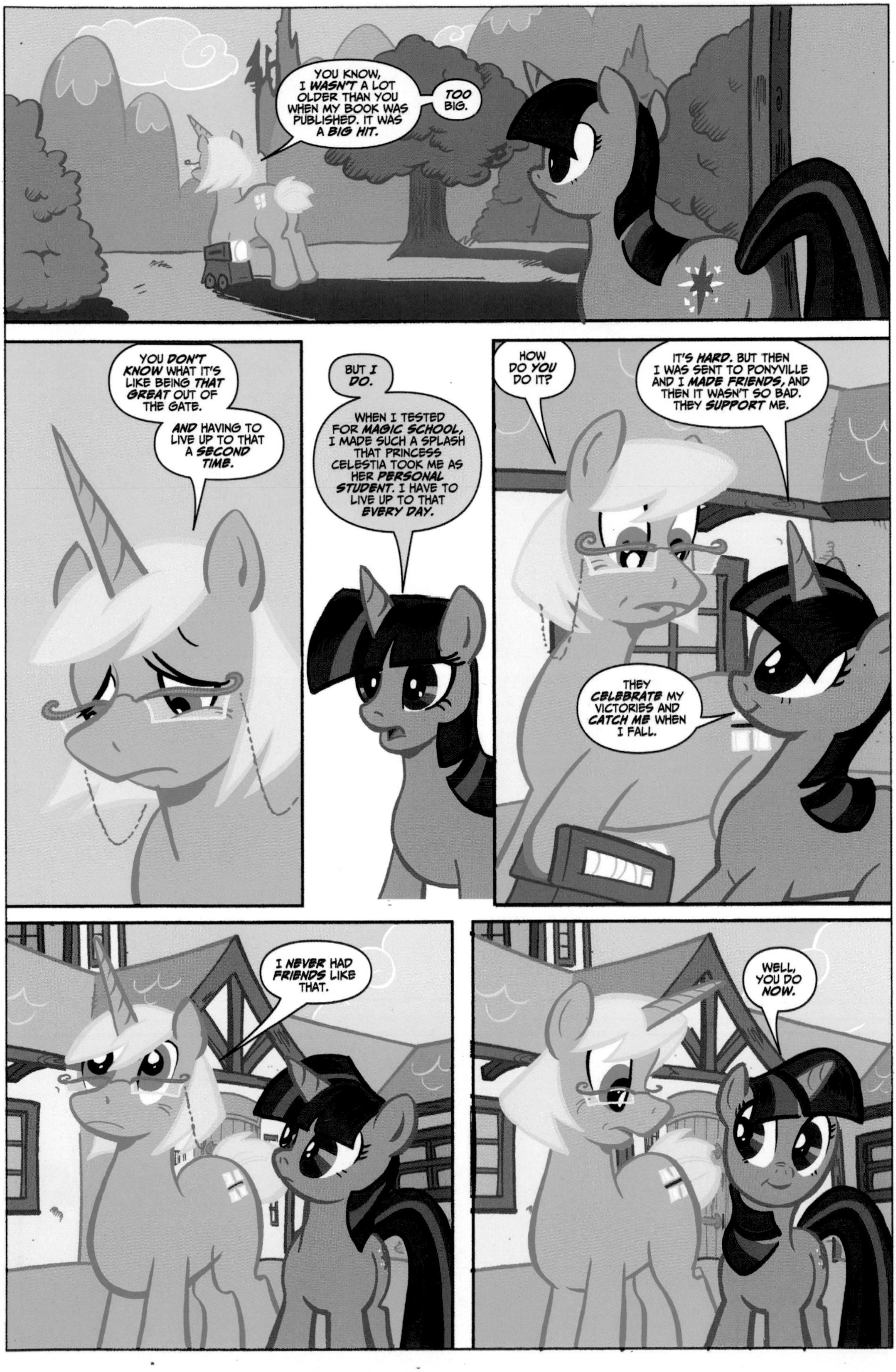

YOU KNOW, I WASN'T A LOT OLDER THAN YOU WHEN MY BOOK WAS PUBLISHED. IT WAS A BIG HIT.
TOO BIG.
YOU DON'T KNOW WHAT IT'S LIKE BEING THAT GREAT OUT OF THE GATE.
AND HAVING TO LIVE UP TO THAT A SECOND TIME.
BUT I DO.
WHEN I TESTED FOR MAGIC SCHOOL, I MADE SUCH A SPLASH THAT PRINCESS CELESTIA TOOK ME AS HER PERSONAL STUDENT. I HAVE TO LIVE UP TO THAT EVERY DAY.
HOW DO YOU DO IT?
IT'S HARD. BUT THEN I WAS SENT TO PONYVILLE AND I MADE FRIENDS, AND THEN IT WASN'T SO BAD. THEY SUPPORT ME.
THEY CELEBRATE MY VICTORIES AND CATCH ME WHEN I FALL.
I NEVER HAD FRIENDS LIKE THAT.
WELL, YOU DO NOW.

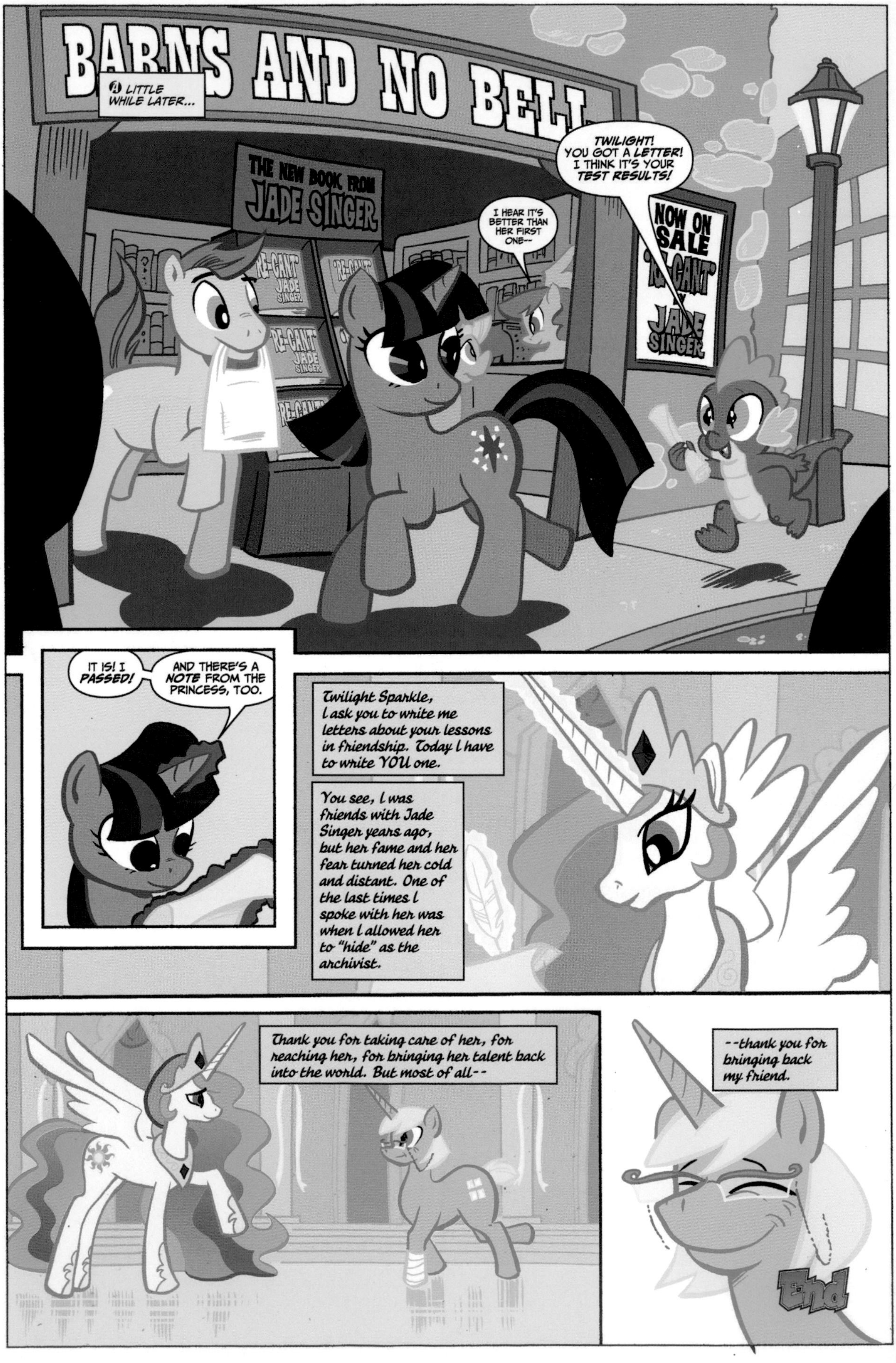
BARNS AND NO BELL
A LITTLE WHILE LATER...
THE NEW BOOK FROM JADE SINGER
RE-GANT JADE SINGER
NOW ON SALE
I HEAR IT'S BETTER THAN HER FIRST ONE--
TWILIGHT! YOU GOT A LETTER! I THINK IT'S YOUR TEST RESULTS!
IT IS! I PASSED!
AND THERE'S A NOTE FROM THE PRINCESS, TOO.
Twilight Sparkle, I ask you to write me letters about your lessons in friendship. Today I have to write YOU one.
You see, I was friends with Jade Singer years ago, but her fame and her fear turned her cold and distant. One of the last times I spoke with her was when I allowed her to "hide" as the archivist.
Thank you for taking care of her, for reaching her, for bringing her talent back into the world. But most of all--
--thank you for bringing back my friend.
End